E
SAR Sargent, Dave
     Biscuit

10094160

Biscuit

By

Dave and Pat Sargent

Illustrated by
Jane Lenoir

Ozark Publishing, Inc.
P.O. Box 228
Prairie Grove, AR 72753

Sargent, Dave, 1941-
    Biscuit / by Dave and Pat Sargent ; illustrated by Jane
Lenoir. — Prairie Grove, AR : Ozark Publishing, ©2001.
    ix, 36 p. : col. ill. ; 23 cm.   (Saddle-up series)

    "Follow rules"—Cover.
    SUMMARY: When British sympathizers steal the mounts
of Washington, Jefferson, and Franklin on the night before
the Constitutional Convention, it is up to Washington's
skewbald horse to plan their escape. Includes factual
information on skewbald horses.
    ISBN: 1-56763-675-6   (hc)
          1-56763-676-4 (pbk)

    1. United States. Constitutional Convention (1787)—
Juvenile fiction. [1. United States. Constitutional Convention
(1787)—Fiction. 2. Horses—Fiction. 3. Washington, George,
1732-1799—Fiction.]   I. Sargent, Pat, 1936- II. Lenoir,
Jane, 1950- ill. III. Title. IV. Series.

    PZ10.3. S243Bis 2001
    [E]—dc21   2001-003042

Printed in the United States of America

iv

Inspired by

the pretty skewbalds we see in fields beside the road as we travel the highways and byways of America.

Dedicated to

all children who love spotted horses.

Foreword

Biscuit is George Washington's mount. Three very important men plan to attend a convention that will decide whether the United States will be independent of both British and French rule.

The men, George Washington, Thomas Jefferson, and Benjamin Franklin, have plans to go to this constitutional convention, but their horses are horsenapped. Can Biscuit think of a plan that will save them?

Contents

One   Biscuit Is Horsenapped!   1

Two   The Hostages Escape   15

Three   The Constitutional Convention   25

Four   Skewbald Facts   35

ix

Biscuit

If you would like to have the authors of the Saddle Up Series visit your school, free of charge, call 1-800-321-5671 or 1-800-960-3876.

One

Biscuit Is Horsenapped!

The western horizon was filled with vivid colors of gold, pink, and lavender as Biscuit Skewbald and his boss walked toward the barn. Both suddenly stopped to look at the beautiful sky.

"Wow wee," Biscuit murmured, "that is one beautiful sunset!"

"This may possibly be an omen, Biscuit," George Washington said quietly. "I will be addressing the Constitutional Convention tomorrow in Philadelphia. I hope it goes well."

Hmmm, the skewbald thought. Sounds as if a bunch of important folks are going to have a big get-together and talk serious business.

The skewbald nuzzled George on the cheek with his upper lip and nickered. "Go for it, Boss. I know you can make good things happen!"

"My colleagues and I are now framing the rules that will govern our new nation," George said.

"New nation?" Biscuit said. "This country is as old as the rest of the world."

"We are now in the process of establishing the United States as an independent country. No more French or British rule over our land. We are going to be our own bosses." He smiled and sighed before adding, "We've been working on this very important document for a long time. Tomorrow we all sign our approval."

"Oh," Biscuit replied with a nod of his head. "Now I understand. It's hard work to have a bunch of folks agree on anything."

George chuckled and patted him on the neck.

"Sometimes I feel that you have the wisdom of a true Federalist."

Two hours later, the barn was quiet, and Biscuit was sound asleep. Suddenly the barn door opened, and a moment later he felt a rough hand tugging on his halter rope.

"Come on, you," a gruff voice ordered. "You're going with us."

"Me?" Biscuit asked. "Wait a minute. My boss didn't tell me to go with you. George Washington has a very important meeting tomorrow." He jerked his head away from the stranger. "I'm not going."

Biscuit felt the sting from a whip on his rump, and he quickly followed the man through the open barn door and into the dark night. For an hour, he trotted and loped beside the black horse of the man.

"Where are we going? Do you know?" he sputtered.

"To a place not far from here," the black replied between clenched teeth. "Sorry about horsenapping you, but if I don't obey him, I'll be in real trouble. Keep up with me.

7

We'll be at the corral pretty soon."

Biscuit did not ask any more questions as they loped through the darkness of the night. Finally they traveled through a grove of trees and stopped in front of a cabin. A big man with a deep voice ran out of the cabin to greet the mean man.

"I have Washington's skewbald horse," he said with an evil laugh. "Where do you want him?"

"Just put him in the corral with the other two," the big man growled. "This skewbald is the last hostage we'll need to stop that convention from meeting tomorrow."

"Hostage?" Biscuit yelled. "Stop the convention? You two are not loyal Americans!"

Before he had a chance to protest further, the mean man took him to the corral and turned him loose to join two other horses. Moments later, after the man left the corral, Biscuit introduced himself to the other hostages. He cleared his throat, straightened his shoulders, and stepped forward.

"I am Biscuit Skewbald." He nickered in a loud, assertive voice. "My boss is George Washington. He's from Mount Vernon, Virginia. And what is your name?" he asked the horse standing nearest to him.

"My name is Sugar Cream," she said quietly. "And my boss is Benjamin Franklin."

"And you?" Biscuit asked as he pointed his front hoof at the other horse.

"I am Popcorn Blue Corn," the horse replied. "My boss is a fine man named Thomas Jefferson."

"Hmmm," the skewbald said. "Are your bosses supposed to be at the Constitutional Convention in the morning?"

The cream and the blue corn both nodded their heads.

"Mine, too," Biscuit said softly. "This is beginning to make sense. These fellows do not want the rules that will govern the new nation to be signed and approved."

The blue corn nodded his head and nickered. "I did overhear them talking about Great Britain and other English stuff on the way here."

"You see, that explains it!" Biscuit shouted. "If they hold us as hostages, our bosses will not get to the convention on time. We have to get out of here and hurry home!"

Two

The Hostages Escape

The skewbald, the blue corn, and the cream paced back and forth in the corral for several minutes without speaking. Suddenly Biscuit heard a familiar voice.

"What are you guys doing? You should be asleep."

"Hi, Black," the skewbald said quietly. "We have a big problem and are trying to find a solution."

"What's your problem?" the black asked. "You have food and water, don't you?"

"I don't know," Biscuit replied with a long sigh. "I'm not hungry or thirsty. Our problem is bigger than that right now."

"Wow!" the black responded. "I didn't know there could be a problem bigger than that."

Sugar Cream walked closer to the black and quietly wiped a tear from her face on one knee.

"My boss, Benjamin Franklin, is also my very best friend. He is depending on me to deliver him to Philadelphia early in the morning." A quiet sob echoed through the night as she added, "But I am a hostage and cannot go home to get him."

The black nodded, then looked at Popcorn Blue Corn and asked, "Who is your boss?"

"T - T - Thomas Jefferson,"

17

Popcorn stuttered. "I have always taken pride in my ability to care for him." He hesitated a moment before adding, "Until now."

"And you?" the black asked Biscuit.

"George Washington is my boss," he said quietly. "I have taken him to meetings for a long time now, and I've never been late." He looked at the black and put his ears against the back of his head. "This will be the first time," he growled.

"Don't get mad at me," the black said as he backed away from the fence. "I'm not holding you three hostage. My bosses are."

"Well," the cream snorted, "you need to find some new bosses."

The black nodded his head in agreement.

"I would if I knew how," he muttered.

Suddenly Biscuit squealed and pounded the ground with one hoof.

"I think I know how," he said.
"Your solution is the same as ours.
We all escape and run away."

"But this place is my home," the black protested. "How can I escape from a bad situation if I'm already home?"

Biscuit stood quietly for a few minutes. Then he smiled and said, "That's easy. You go home with me, and I will find you a nice boss."

"That sounds wonderful," the black agreed. "Let's do it!"

Twenty minutes later, Biscuit was leading the cream, the blue corn, and the black through the trees toward the road.

"We must hurry," he shouted over his shoulder. "It will be daylight soon, and we must be home in time to deliver our bosses to the Constitutional Convention."

He heard murmurs of agreement from two of his friends as they thundered through the darkness of pre-dawn.

"What about me?" Black asked. "Why should I hurry? No one cares where I am or what I'm doing, except my mean boss." He was quiet for a moment before chuckling, "And he's not my boss anymore. Let's go home, wherever it is!"

Three

The Constitutional Convention

The sun was peeking over the eastern horizon when the skewbald and the black arrived at the barn. George Washington was pacing back and forth with his hands clasped behind his back.

"Hi, Boss!" Biscuit nickered as he came to a halt beside him. "The cream and the blue corn will deliver Mr. Franklin and Mr. Jefferson to the meeting on time. In spite of the British bad guys, we're all going to arrive on time!"

George frowned at Biscuit and said, "Where in the world have you been? If we don't leave right now, I'll be late for the convention."

The black nickered softly and a tear trickled down his face.

"I'm sorry," George apologized. "I was not scolding you. Where is your home? Maybe Biscuit and I can take you home after the meeting. Would that make you feel better?"

The skewbald chuckled as the black shook his head and pawed the ground with one front hoof.

"Don't you worry," Biscuit said soothingly. "You can travel with us. I'll explain everything to Boss later."

Suddenly Biscuit saw a man walking up the lane toward them. He approached George Washington and shook his hand.

"Forgive me for bothering you, George," he said breathlessly, "but my horse is not feeling well today. Do you have one that I may borrow?"

"James Madison, my friend," George said, "I would certainly help you if I had another horse."

27

Biscuit squealed and pawed the ground. He pointed one front hoof at the black.

"Boss!" he yelled. "Here is the perfect horse for Mr. Madison."

The black proudly trotted up to James Madison and stopped in front of him. His head was held high, and his ears were alert and forward.

"Hmmm," George said. "Well, my friend. Perhaps there is a horse available for you."

He stroked the neck of the black and looked at James. Biscuit nodded his head and smiled.

"You're right, Boss," he said. "The black needs a good home, and Mr. James Madison needs a horse. The two are a perfect match!"

By late afternoon in May 1787, the Constitution of the United States was adopted by the members of the Constitutional Convention. Biscuit, Sugar Cream, Popcorn, and the black peeked through the windows of the meeting hall to watch their bosses sign the powerful and all-important document.

Biscuit smiled and sighed with pride and pleasure as he watched his boss lead the United States up the path to become a strong, successful nation.

"Wow," the black said quietly. "You said you would help me find a new home, Biscuit. But you did not tell me that my first job with my new boss would be a historical landmark in time!"

"Neat, huh?" Biscuit snorted. "Good things are happening all over the place."

Later that evening as George was unsaddling Biscuit, he leaned over and whispered a secret to the skewbald.

"Biscuit, my trusty friend," he said. "We have a new independent nation, and one day very soon, our country will need a leader. Perhaps I will be considered."

The skewbald nodded his head.

"I think you would make a fine leader of the United States, Boss," he said quietly. "You are honest, trustworthy, and loyal. I would call you the perfect man for the job!"

Moments later, George left the barn, and Biscuit was alone to savor the memory of this special day.

"Those men," he murmured, "who attended the convention will be spoken of in history books. There will be artists who draw pictures of them signing the Constitution. But I can't help but wonder if they will tell the whole story. They won't even know about the British bad guys or the horsenapping or the scary hostage situation."

Hmmmmm, he thought. They won't even remember good old Biscuit Skewbald or Sugar Cream or

Popcorn Blue Corn or the runaway black. But I don't mind. My boss may become the very first president of the United States, and that is truly wonderful. Life is good and it just gets better and better!

Four

Skewbald Facts

Skewbald is the term used to describe horses having asymmetrical white patterns. The patches usually involve well-defined areas of solid white.

The term *skewbald* originated in Britain, where white spotting is rare on horses. It is more accurate to state the background color of the horse and then the specific pattern that is present.

The word *skewbald* refers to a nonblack horse with patterns of white. In other words, the horse can be any color, with white patches; That is, any color except black.

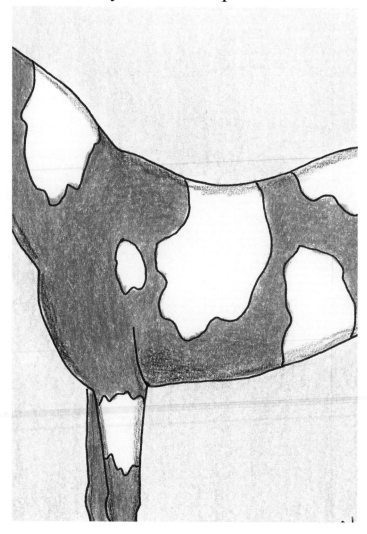

E
SAR Sargent, Dave
Biscuit

10094160